To my mother, with love.
KW

To my niece, Gwen.
PM

Text copyright © Karen Wallace 1996
Illustrations copyright © Peter Melnyczuk 1996

The right of Karen Wallace and Peter Melnyczuk to be identified
as the author and illustrator of the work has been asserted by them in
accordance with the copyright, Designs and Patents Act 1988

Published by Hodder Children's Books 1996

Printed and bound by Oriental Press, Dubai

10 9 8 7 6 5 4 3

Hardback ISBN 0 340 63435 9
Paperback ISBN 0 340 65134 2

Hodder Children's Books
A division of Hodder Headline plc
338 Euston Road
London NW1 3BH

Imagine you are a
TIGER

Written by Karen Wallace

Illustrated by Peter Melnyczuk

Hodder
Children's
Books

Imagine you are a tiger.

A tiny tiger is born in a den on dry grass.

His eyes are tight shut and he mews like a kitten.

He scrambles through his mother's fur and finds her milk.

The tiny tiger sucks until his belly is full.

Imagine you are a tiger.

A little tiger creeps from his den.

His eyes are open now.

He sees a green parakeet flutter from a tree.

He sees a black-faced monkey jump in the branches.

He hears quick steps behind him.

His mother is standing over him.

The stripes on her fur look like shadows on the ground.

She picks up the little tiger and holds him in her jaws.

He hangs floppy as a ragdoll

as she carries him back to the den.

Imagine you are a tiger.

A young tiger grows quickly.

He wrestles with his brother.

He snarls and bares his teeth.

He pounces and pulls his brother to the ground.

Soon the young tiger will hunt in the forest.

The sun is high in the sky. The air is hot and dusty.

The young tiger follows his mother down to the river.

He watches her wallow in the water.

He sits on the shore, wanting to be with her.

A young tiger learns to swim quickly.

He leaps and splashes with his brother.

Then he lies in the shade
and watches the river through half-closed eyes.

Deer come.

They stand on flat rocks and drink in the sun.

They are frightened of the tigers.

But the flat rocks burn like oven plates.

They are too hot for tigers' paws.

The deers' hooves keep them safe.

Wild boar come.

They grunt and jostle by the water.

They hide their piglets under a thorny bush.

They are frightened of the tigers.

The boars' tusks are sharp. Their skin is tough as old leather.

But their piglets are fatty and sweet.

Imagine you are a tiger.

A young tiger sees his mother steal from the water.

She leaps through the shade to the thorny bush.

And snatches a piglet.

The young tiger runs with his brother after his mother.
Over the grassland and into the forest.

She gives them the piglet and lies down beside them.
A hungry young tiger eats as much as he can.

Imagine you are a tiger.

A fierce full-grown tiger strides through the long grass.

His stripes look like stalks.

His gold fur shines like sun on the ground.

He sees a deer on her own.

He crawls on his belly, ready to spring.

A black-faced monkey screams in a treetop.

The deer hears his warning and gallops away.

A cunning tiger crouches in the grass.

He waits and listens.

He hears hoofbeats thud on the hard ground.

He peers through the grass with clear yellow eyes.

An antelope is crossing the scrubland towards him.

Imagine you are a tiger.